The Talking Thrush
and
Other Folk-Tales

"A Crow is a Crow for ever."

The Talking Thrush

and

Other Folk-Tales

Collected by
W. CROOKE

Retold by
W. H. D. ROUSE

Illustrated by
W. H. ROBINSON

HAWK PRESS

Published by

Hawk Press
4836/24, Ansari Road, Daryaganj
New Delhi – 110 002
Phones : 9643330713, +91-11-23278618, +91-11-35676207
E-mail : thehawkpress@gmail.com
www.thehawkpress.com

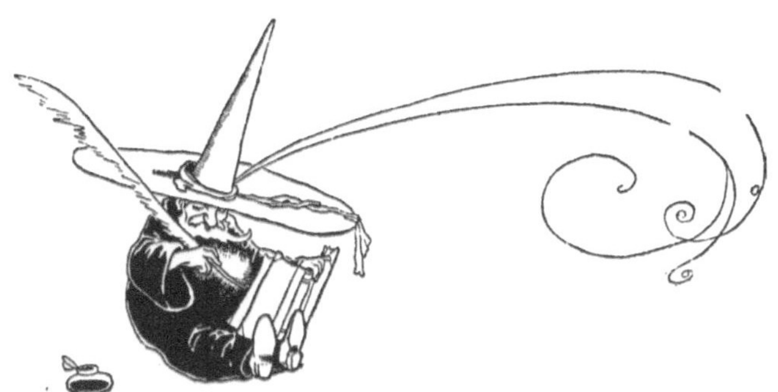

Contents

Preface

THE stories contained in this little book are only a small part of a large collection of Indian folk-tales, made by Mr. Crooke in the course of the Ethnological Survey of the North-West Provinces and Oudh. Some were recorded by the collector from the lips of the jungle-folk of Mirzápur; others by his native assistant, Pandit Rámgharíb Chaubé. Besides these, a large number were received from all parts of the Provinces in response to a circular issued by Mr. J. C. Nesfield, the Director of Public Instruction, to all teachers of village schools.

The present selection is confined to the Beast Stories, which are particularly interesting as being mostly indigenous and little affected by so-called Aryan influence. Most of them are new, or have been published only in the *North Indian Notes and Queries*.

In the re-telling, for which Mr. Rouse is responsible, a number of changes have been made. The text of the book is meant for children, and consequently the first aim has been to make an interesting story. Those who study folk-tales for any scientific purpose will find all such changes marked in the Notes. If the change is considerable, the original document is summarised. It should be added that these documents are merely brief Notes in themselves, without literary interest. The Notes also give the source of each tale, and a few obvious parallels, or references to the literature of the subject.

The Talking Thrush

A Certain man had a garden, and in his garden he sowed cotton seeds. By-and-by the cotton seeds grew up into a cotton bush, with big brown pods upon it. These pods burst open when they are ripe; and you can see the fluffy white cotton bulging all white out of the pods. There was a Thrush in this garden, and the Thrush thought within herself how nice and soft the cotton looked. She plucked out some of it to line her nest with; and never before was her sleep so soft as it was on that bed of cotton.

Now this Thrush had a clever head; so she thought something more might be done with cotton besides lining a nest. In her flights abroad she used often to pass by the door of a Cotton-carder. The Cotton-carder had a thing like a bow, made of a piece of wood, and a thong of leather tying the ends together into a curve. He used to take the cotton, and pile it in a heap; then he took the carding-bow, and twang-twang-twanged it among the heap of cotton, so that the fibres or threads of it became disentangled. Then he rolled it up into oblong balls, and sold it to other people, who made it into thread.

The Thrush often watched the Cotton-carder at work. Every day after dinner, she went to the cotton tree, and plucked out a fluff of cotton in her beak and hid it away. She went on doing this till at last she had quite a little heap of cotton all of her own. At least, it was not really her own, because she stole it; but then you cannot get policemen to take up a Thrush for stealing, and as men catch Thrushes and put them in a cage all for nothing, it is only fair the birds should have their turn.

When the heap of cotton was big enough, our Thrush flew to the house of the Cotton-carder, and sat down in front of him.

"Good day, Man," said the Thrush.

"Good day, Birdie," said the Cotton-carder. The Thrush was not a bit afraid, because she knew he was a kind man, who never caught little birds to put them in a cage. He liked better to hear them singing free in the woods.

"Man," said the Thrush, "I have a heap of beautiful cotton, and I'll tell you what. You shall have half of it, if you will card the rest and make it up into balls for me."

"That I will," said the man; "where is it?"

"If you will come with me," said the Thrush, "I'll show you."

So the Thrush flew in front, and the man followed after, and they came to the place where the hoard of cotton was hidden away. The man took the cotton home, and carded it, and made it into balls. Half of the cotton he took for his trouble, and the rest he gave back to the Thrush. He was so honest that he did not cheat even a bird, although he could easily have done so. For birds cannot count: and if you find a nest full of eggs, and take one or two, the mother-bird will never miss them; but if you take all, the bird is unhappy.

Not far away from the Carder lived a Spinner. This man used to put a ball of cotton on a stick, and then he pulled out a bit of the cotton without breaking it, and tied it to another little stick with a weight on it. Then he twisted the weight, and set it a-spinning; and as it span, he held the cotton ball in one hand, and pulled out the cotton with the other, working it between finger and thumb to keep it fine. Thus the spindle went on spinning, and the cotton went on twisting, until it was twisted into thread. That is why the man was called a Spinner. It looks very easy to do, when you can do it; but it is really very hard to do well.

To this Spinner the Thrush came, and after bidding him good day, said she--

"Mr. Spinner, I have some balls of cotton all ready to spin into thread. Will you spin one half of them into thread for me, if I give you the other half?"

"That I will," said Mr. Spinner; and away they went to find the cotton balls, Thrush first and Spinner following.

In a very few days the Spinner had spun all the cotton into the finest thread. Then he took a pair of scales, and weighed it into two equal parts (he was an honest man, too): half he kept for himself, and the other half he gave to the Thrush.

The next thing this clever Thrush did was to fly to the house of a Weaver. The Weaver used to buy thread, and fasten a number of threads to a wooden frame, called a loom, which was made of two upright posts, with another bar fastened across the top. The threads were hung to the cross-bar, and a little stone was tied to the bottom of each, to keep it steady. Then the Weaver wound some more thread around a long stick called a shuttle; and the shuttle he pushed in front of one thread and behind the next, until it had gone right across the whole of the threads, in and out. Then he pushed it back in the same way, and after a bit, the upright threads and the cross-threads were woven together and made a piece of cloth.

The Thrush flew down to the Weaver, and they made the same bargain as before. The Weaver wove all the thread into pieces of cloth, and half he kept for himself, but the other half he returned to the Thrush.

So now the Thrush had some beautiful cloth, and I dare say you wonder what she wanted it for. As you have not been inquisitive, I will tell you: she wanted clothes to dress herself. The Thrush had noticed that men and women walking about wore clothes, and being an ambitious Thrush, and eager to rise in the world, she felt it would not be proper to go about without any clothes on. So she now went to a Tailor, and said to him--

"Good Mr. Tailor, I have some pieces of very fine cloth, and I should be much obliged if you would make a part of it into clothes for me. You shall have one half of the cloth for your trouble."

The Tailor was very glad of this job, as times were slack. So he took the cloth, and at once set to work. Half of it he made into a beautiful dress for the Thrush, with a skirt and jacket, and sleeves in the latest fashion; and as there was a little cloth left over, and he was an honest Tailor, he made her also a pretty little hat to put on her head.

Then the Thrush was indeed delighted, and felt there was little more to desire in the world. She put on her skirt, and her jacket with fashionable sleeves, and the little hat, and looked at her image in a river, and was mightily pleased with herself. Now she became so vain that nothing would do, but she must show herself to the King.

So she flew and flew, and away she flew, until she came to the King's palace. Into the King's palace she flew, and into the great hall where the King sat and the Queen and all the courtiers. There was a peg high up on the wall, and the Thrush perched on this peg, and began to sing.

"Oh, look there!" cried the Queen, who was the first to see this wonderful sight--"see, a Thrush in a jacket and skirt and a pretty hat!"

Everybody looked at the Thrush singing on her peg, and clapped their hands.

"Come here, Birdie," said the King, "and show the Queen your pretty clothes."

The Thrush felt highly flattered, and flew down upon the table, and took off her jacket to show the Queen. Then she flew back to her peg, and watched to see what would happen.

The Queen turned over the jacket in her hand, and laughed. Then she folded it up, and put it in her pocket.

"Give me my jacket!" twittered the Thrush. "I shall catch cold, and besides, it is not proper for a lady to be seen without a jacket."

Then they all laughed, and the King said, "Come here, Mistress Thrush, and you shall have your jacket."

Down flew the Thrush upon the table again; but the King caught her, and held her fast.

"Let me go!" squeaked the Thrush, struggling to get free.

But the King would not let her go. I am afraid that although he was a King, he was not so honest as the Carder or the Spinner, and cared less for his word than the Weaver and the Tailor.

"Greedy King," said the Thrush, "to covet my little jacket!"

"I covet more than your jacket," said the King; "I covet you, and I am going to chop you up into little bits."

Then he began to chop her up into bits. As she was being chopped up, the Thrush said, "The King snips and cuts like a Tailor, but he is not so honest!"

When the King had finished chopping her up, he began to wash the pieces. And each piece, as he washed it, called out, "The King scours and scrubs like a washerwoman, but he is not so honest!"

Then the King put the pieces of the Thrush into a frying-pan with oil, and began to fry them. But the pieces went on calling out, "The King is like a cook, frying and sputtering, but he is not so honest!"

When she was fried, the King ate her up. From within the body of the King still the Thrush kept calling out, "I am inside the King! It is just like the inside of any other man, only not so honest!"

The King became like a walking musical-box, and he did not like it at all, but it was his own fault. Wherever he went, everybody heard the Thrush crying out from inside the King, "Just like any other man, only not so honest!" Everybody that heard this began to despise the King.

At last the King could stand it no longer. He sent for his doctor, and said, "Doctor, you must cut this talking bird out of me."

"Your majesty will die, if I do," said the Doctor.

"I shall die if you don't," answered the King, "for I cannot endure being made a fool of."

So there was nothing for it: the Doctor took his knives, and made a hole in the King, and pulled out theThrush. Strange to say, the pieces of the Thrush had all joined together again, and away she flew; but her beautiful clothes were all gone. However, it was a lesson she never forgot; and after that, she slept soft in her nest of cotton, and never again tried to ape her betters. As for the King, he died; and a good riddance too. His son became king in his stead; and all life long he remembered his father's miserable death, and kept all his promises to men, and beasts, and birds.

The Rabbit and the Monkey

Once upon a time, there lived in the mountains a Rabbit and a Monkey, who were great friends. One day, as they sat by the roadside hobnobbing together, who should come by but a man with a bamboo pole over his shoulder, and at each end of the pole was a bundle hung to a string; and there were plantains in one bundle, and sugar in the other.

Said the Monkey to the Rabbit, "Friend of my heart, do as I shall tell you. Go and sit upon the road in front of that man, and as soon as he sees you, run--he is sure to drop his load and follow. Then I will pick up his load, and hide it safely; and when you come back, we will share it together."

No sooner said than done: the Rabbit ran, and the man dropped his burden and ran after him; while the Monkey, who had been hiding in the tall grass by the wayside, pounced upon the sugar and the plantains, and
climbed up into a tree, and began to gobble them up at his leisure.

By-and-by the man came back, hot and empty-handed, and finding that his goods were gone as well as the Rabbit, cursed loudly, and went home to be scolded by his wife.

Soon the Rabbit came back too, and began hunting about for his friend the Monkey. High and low he searched, and not a trace could he find; till he happened to cast his eyes aloft, and lo and behold, there was Mr. Monkey up in a tree, munching away with every sign of enjoyment.

"Hullo, friend," said he, "come down out of that."

"I'm very comfortable here, thank you," said the Monkey.

"But where's my share?" asked the Rabbit indignantly.

"All gone, all gone," mumbled the Monkey, and pelted him with the plantain-peel and balls of paper made out of the packets where the sugar had been. "Why did you stay so long? I got hungry, and could not wait any longer."

The Rabbit thought his friend was joking, and would not believe it; but it was only too true--the greedy creature had not left a scrap.
"Do you really mean it?" said the poor Rabbit.

"If you don't believe me, come and see," said the Monkey, and seizing the Rabbit by his long ears, he hauled him up into the tree; and after mocking him, and making great game, he left him there, and went away.

Now the Rabbit was afraid to jump down from such a height, for fear of breaking his neck, so up in the tree he remained for a long time. Many animals passed under the tree, but none took pity on the rabbit, until at last came an old and foolish Rhinoceros, who rubbed his withered hide against the trunk.
"Kind Rhinoceros," said the Rabbit, "let me jump down upon your back."

The Rhinoceros, being a simple creature, agreed. Down came the Rabbit, with such a thud, that the Rhinoceros fell on his stupid old nose, and broke his fat old neck, and died.

The Rabbit ran away, and away he ran, until he came to the King's palace; and he hid under the King's golden throne. By-and-by in came the King, and in came the court; all the grandees stood around in their golden robes, glittering with rubies and diamonds, and their swords were girt about their waists. Suddenly they all heard a terrific sneeze!

Everybody said, "God bless you," while the King thundered out: "Who has the bad manners to sneeze in the King's presence?" Everybody looked at his neighbour, and wondered who did it. "Off with his head," shouted the King.

Another sneeze came. This time, however, everybody was on the watch, and they noticed that the sound came from under the King's golden throne. So they dived in, and lugged out the Rabbit, looking more dead than alive.

"All right," said the King, "off with his head." The executioner ran to get his sword.

But our friend the Rabbit, for all he was frightened, had his wits about him; and sitting up on his hind-legs, and putting his two fore-paws together, he said respectfully, "O great King, strike, but hear. If thou wilt send a score of men with me, I will give thee a dead Rhinoceros."

The King laughed, the courtiers laughed loud and long. However, just to see what would come of it, the King gave him a score of men.

The Rabbit led them to the place where the Rhinoceros fell on his stupid old nose, and there he lay dead. With great difficulty the men dragged the Rhinoceros home. They were very pleased to get a Rhinoceros, because his horn is good for curing many diseases, and the court physician ground his horn into powder, and made out of it a most wonderful medicine. And the King was so pleased, that he gave the Rabbit a fine new coat, and a horse to ride on.

So the Rabbit put on his fine coat, and got on the back of his horse, and rode off.

On the way, who should meet him but his friend the Monkey.

"Hullo!" says the Monkey, "where did you get all that finery?"

"The King gave it to me," says the Rabbit.

Says the Monkey, "And why should the King give all this to a fool like
you?"

The Rabbit replied, "I, whom you call a fool, got it by sneezing under the King's golden throne; such a lucky sneeze, that the soothsayers prophesied to the King long life and many sons!" Then he rode away.

The Monkey fell a-thinking how nice it would be if he could get a fine coat and horse as the Rabbit had done. "I can sneeze," thought he; "what if I try my luck?"

So he scampered away, and away he scampered, till he came to the King's palace, and hid himself under the King's golden throne. When the King came in, and all his courtiers, in gorgeous array as before, our Monkey underneath the throne sneezed in the most auspicious manner he could contrive.

"Who is that?" thundered the King, glaring about him. "Who has the bad manners to sneeze in the King's presence?"

They searched about until they found the Monkey hidden under the throne, and hauled him out.

"What hast thou, wily tree-climber," asked the King, "that I should not bid the executioner cut off thy head?"

The monkey had no answer ready. At last he said, "O King, I have some plantain-peel and pellets of paper." But the King was angry at this, and the greedy Monkey was led away, and his head was cut off.

The Sparrow's Revenge

nce there was a pair of Sparrows that were very fond of each other, and lived in a nest together as happy as the day was long. The hen laid eggs and sat upon them, and the cock went about picking up food for them both, and when he had got food enough, he sat on a twig close by the nest, and twittered for joy.

But it happened one day that a boy saw Cock Sparrow pecking at some seeds, and he picked up a stone and threw it at him, and killed him. So no food came home that morning, and Hen Sparrow grew anxious, and at last set out to find him.

In a little while she found his dead body lying in a ditch. She ruffled up her feathers and began to cry. "Who can have killed him?" she said; "my poor kind husband, who never did harm to any one." Then a Raven flew down from a tree, where he had been sitting, and told her how a cruel boy had thrown a stone at him and killed him for sport. He saw it, said the Raven, as he was sitting on the tree.

Now Hen Sparrow determined to have her revenge. She was so much troubled that she left her eggs to hatch themselves, or to

addle if they would; and gathering some straw, she plaited it into a beautiful straw carriage, with two old cotton-reels for wheels, and sticks for the
shafts. Then she went to the hole of a Rat who was a friend of hers, and called down the hole, "Mr. Rat! Mr. Rat!"

"Yes, Mrs. Sparrow," said the Rat, coming out of the hole and making a polite bow.

"Some one has thrown a stone at my husband and killed him. Will you help me to get my revenge?"

"Why," said the Rat, "how can I help you?"

"By pulling me along in my carriage," said Mrs. Sparrow.

"Oh yes," said the Rat; "that I will." So he went down into his hole again, and washed his face, and combed his whiskers, and came up all spick and span.
Mrs. Sparrow tied the shafts of the straw carriage to the Rat, and Mrs. Sparrow got in, and off they went.

On the road they met a Scorpion. Said the Scorpion--

"Whither away, Mrs. Sparrow and Mr. Rat?"

Said the Hen Sparrow, "My friend Mr. Rat is pulling me along in my carriage of straw to punish a cruel boy who threw a stone at my husband and killed him."

"Quite right too," said the Scorpion. "May I come and help you? I have a beautiful sting in my tail."

"Oh, please do! come and get in," said the Sparrow.

In got the Scorpion, and away they went. By-and-by they saw a Snake.

"Good day, and God bless you," says the Snake. "Where are you going, may a mere reptile ask?"

"Mr. Scorpion and I are going to punish a cruel boy who threw a stone and killed my husband."

"Shall I come and help you?" asked the Snake. "I have fine teeth in my head to bite with."

"The more the merrier," replied Mrs. Sparrow. So in he got. They had not gone far before who should meet them but a Wolf.

"Hullo," says the Wolf gruffly; "where are you off to, I should like to know?"

"Mr. Rat is kind enough to draw me in my carriage, and we are all going to punish a cruel boy who threw a stone and killed my poor husband."

"May I come too?" growled the Wolf. "I can bite." He opened his big jaws and snarled.

"Oh, how kind you are!" said Mrs. Sparrow. "Do come! jump in, jump in!"

The poor Rat looked aghast at such a load to pull; but he was a gentlemanly Rat, and so, having offered to pull the carriage, he said nothing.

So the big Wolf got in, and nearly sat on the Scorpion's tail; if he had, he wouldn't have sat long, I think. However, the Scorpion got out of the way, and on they went all four, the poor Rat pulling with all his might, but rather slow at that.

In due time they arrived at the cruel boy's house. His mother was cooking the dinner, and his father was fast asleep in a chair. There was a river close by the house, and the Wolf went down to the river, and hid himself there; the Snake crawled among the peats, and the Scorpion began to climb up into the chair where the man was sleeping.

Then Mrs. Hen Sparrow flew in at the door and twittered--

"Little boy! Little boy! There's a fish biting at your night-line!"

Up jumped the boy, and out he ran, to look at the night-line.

But as he was stooping down and looking at the line to see if any fish were hooked, the Wolf pounced upon him, and bit him in the throat, and he died.

Then the cruel boy's mother went out to get some peats, and as she put her hand in amongst them, the Snake bit her, and she gave a shriek and fell down and died. The shriek awoke her husband sleeping in his chair, and he began to get up, but by this time the Scorpion had climbed up the leg of the chair, so he stung the man, and the man died too.

Thus there was an end of the cruel boy who killed a harmless Sparrow for sport; and though his father and mother had done nothing, yet they ought not to have had a son so cruel, or, at least, they might have brought him up better. Anyhow, die they did, all three; and Mrs. Hen Sparrow was so delighted that she forgot all about her dead husband, and forgot her eggs which were getting addled, and went about chirruping until she found another husband, and made another nest, and (I am sorry to say) lived happily ever after.

The Judgment of the Jackal

A was returning home from a long journey, riding upon a mule. As he drew near home, night overtook him; and he was forced to look out for shelter. Seeing a mill by the roadside, he knocked at the door.

"Come in!" said the Miller.

"May I stay here for the night?" asked the Merchant.

"By all means," said the Miller, "if you pay me well."

The Merchant thought this rather mean; because in those days a stranger was made welcome everywhere without paying anything. However, he made the best of it, and came in. The Miller led off his mule to the stable.

"Please take care of my mule," said the Merchant; "I have still a long way to go."

"Oh," said the Miller, "your mule will be all right." Then he rubbed him down and fed him.

In the morning the Merchant asked for his mule.

"I am very sorry," said the Miller; "he must have got loose last night, and I can't find him anywhere."

The Merchant was much dismayed. He went out to look for himself, and there, to be sure, was his mule, tied by the halter to the mill.

"Why, look here, Miller," says he, "here is the mule!"

"Oh no," says the Miller, "that mule is mine."

"Yours?" said the Merchant, getting angry. "Last night your stable was empty. And don't you think I know my own mule?"

"That is mine," said the Miller again; "my mill had a young mule in the night, and that is he."

The Merchant was now very angry indeed; but he could not help himself, as he did not want to fight; he was a very peaceful Merchant. So he said--
"Well, I have no doubt it's all right; but just to satisfy me, let us ask the Rev. Dr. Jackal to decide between us; and whatever he says I will abide by."

"Very good," answered the Miller; and away they went to the den of his reverence the Jackal. Dr. Jackal was sitting with his hind legs crossed, and smoking a hubble-bubble.

"Good morning, worthy gentlemen," said the Jackal; "how can I serve you?"

Said the Merchant, "Last night, my Lord Judge, I lodged with this Miller here, and he took charge of my mule; but now he says it has run away, though I saw it with my own eyes tied by the halter to his mill. He says that the mule I saw is his, and that his mill is the mother of it, and that it was born last night while I was asleep."

"Go back to the mill," said the Jackal, "and wait for me. I will just wash my face, and then I'll settle your business."

They went away, and waited a long time, but no Jackal. Late in the afternoon, they got tired of waiting for the Jackal, and determined to go and look for him. There he was still, sitting in his den and smoking a hubble-bubble.

"Why didn't you come?" asked the Miller. "We have been waiting for you all day."

"Oh, my dear sir, I was too busy," said the Jackal. "When I went to wash my face, I found that all the water had caught fire; I have only just put it out."

"You must be mad, your reverence," said the Miller. "Who ever heard of water catching fire?"

"And who ever heard," replied the Jackal, "of a mill having a young mule?"

The Miller saw that he was found out, and was so much ashamed that he gave back the mule to its owner, and the Merchant went home.

How the Mouse got into his Hole

A MERCHANT was going along the road one day with a sack of peas on the back of an Ox. The Ox was stung by a Fly, and gave a kick, and down fell the sack. A Mouse was passing by, and the Merchant said, "Mousie, if you will help me up with this sack I will give you a pea." The Mouse helped him up with the sack and got a pea for his trouble. He stole another, and a third he found on the road.

When he got home with his three peas he planted them in front of his hole. As he was planting them he said to them, "If you are not all three sprouting by to-morrow I'll cut you in pieces and give you to the black Ox." The peas were terribly frightened, and the next morning they had already begun to sprout, and each of them had two shoots. Then he said,
"If I don't find you in blossom to-morrow I'll cut you in pieces and give you to the black Ox." When he went to look next day they were all in blossom. So he said, "If I don't find ripe peas on you to-morrow I'll cut you in pieces and give you to the black Ox." Next day they had pods full of ripe peas on them.

So every day he used to eat lots of peas, and in this manner he got very fat. One day a pretty young lady Mouse came to see him.

"Good morning, Sleekie," said she; "how are you?"
"Good morning, Squeakie," said he; "I'm quite well, thank you."
"Why, Sleekie," said she, "how fat you are."
"Am I?" said he. "I suppose that's because I have plenty to eat."
"What do you eat, Sleekie?" asked the pretty young lady Mouse.
"Peas, Squeakie," said the other.
"Where do you get them, Sleekie?"
"They grow all of themselves in my garden, Squeakie."
"Will you give me some, please?" asked the lady Mouse.
"Oh yes, if you will stay in my garden, you may have as many as youlike."

So Squeakie stayed in Sleekie's garden, and they both ate so many peas that they got fatter and fatter every day.

One day Squeakie said to Sleekie, "Let's try which can get into the hole quickest." Squeakie was slim, and she had not been at the peas so long as Sleekie, so she got into the hole easily enough; but Sleekie was so fat that he could not get in at all.

He was very much frightened, and went off in hot haste to the Carpenter, and said to him, "Carpenter, please pare off a little flesh from my ribs, so that I can get into my hole."

"Do you think I have nothing better to do than paring down your ribs?" said the Carpenter angrily, and went on with his work.

The Mouse went to the King, and said, "O King, I can't get into my hole, and the Carpenter will not pare down my ribs; will you make him do it?"

"Get out," said the King; "do you think I have nothing better to do than look after your ribs?"

So the Mouse went to the Queen. Said he, "Queen, I can't get into my hole, and the King won't tell the Carpenter to pare down my ribs. Please divorce him."

"Bother you and your ribs," said the Queen; "I am not going to divorce my husband because you have made yourself fat by eating too much."

The Mouse went to the Snake. "Snake, bite the Queen, and tell her to divorce the King, because he will not tell the Carpenter to pare my ribs down and let me get into my hole."

"Get away," said the Snake; "or I'll swallow you up, ribs and all; the fatter you are, the better I shall be pleased."

He went to the Stick, and said, "Stick, beat the Snake, because she won't bite the Queen, who won't divorce the King and make him tell the Carpenter to pare down my ribs, and let me get into my hole."

"Off with you," said the Stick; "I'm sleepy, because I have just beaten a thief; I can't be worried about your ribs."

He went to the Furnace, and said, "Furnace, burn the Stick, and make it beat the Snake, that he may bite the Queen and make her divorce the King, who won't tell the Carpenter to pare down my ribs, and let me get into my hole."

"Get along with you," said the Furnace; "I am cooking the King's dinner, and I have no time now to see about your ribs."

He went to the Ocean, and said, "Ocean, put out the Fire, and make it burn the Stick, so that it may beat the Snake, and the Snake may bite the Queen, and she may divorce the King, who won't tell the Carpenter to pare down my ribs, and let me get into my hole."

"Don't bother me," said the Ocean; "it's high tide, and all the fishes are jumping about, and giving me no rest."

He went to the Elephant, and said, "O Elephant, drink up the Ocean, that it may put out the Fire, and the Fire may burn the Stick, and the Stick may beat the Snake, and the Snake may bite the Queen, and the Queen may
divorce the King, and make him tell the Carpenter to pare down my ribs, and let me get into my hole."

"Go away, little Mouse," said the Elephant; "I have just drunk up a whole lake, and I really can't drink any more."

He went to the Creeper, and said, "Dear Creeper, do please choke the Elephant, that he may drink up the Ocean, and the Ocean may put out the Fire, and the Fire may burn the Stick, and the Stick may beat the Snake, and the Snake may bite the Queen, and the Queen may divorce the King, and the King may tell the Carpenter to pare down my ribs, and let me get into my hole."

"Not I," says the Creeper; "I am stuck fast here to this tree, and I couldn't get away to please a fat little Mouse."

Then he went to the Scythe, and said, "Scythe, please cut loose the Creeper, that it may choke the Elephant, and the Elephant may drink up the Ocean, and the Ocean may put out the Fire, and the Fire may burn the Stick, and the Stick may beat the Snake, and the Snake may bite the Queen, and the Queen may divorce the King, and the King may tell the Carpenter to pare down my ribs, and let me get into my hole."

"With pleasure," said the Scythe, who is always sharp.

So the Scythe cut the Creeper loose, and the Creeper began to choke the Elephant, and the Elephant ran off and began to drink up the Ocean, and the Ocean began to put out the Fire, and the Fire began to burn the Stick, and the Stick began to beat the Snake, and the Snake began to bite the Queen, and the Queen told the King she was going to divorce him, and the King was frightened, and ordered the Carpenter to pare Sleekie's ribs, and at last Sleekie got into his hole.

King Solomon and the Owl

NCE King Solomon was hunting all alone in the forest. Night fell, and King Solomon lay down under a tree to sleep. Over his head, on the branch of a tree, sat a huge Owl; and the Owl hooted so loud and so long, Too-whit too-woo! Too-whit too-woo! that Solomon could not sleep. Solomon looked up at the Owl, and said--

"Tell me, O Owl, why do you hoot all night long upon the trees?"

Said the Owl--

> "I hoot to waken those that sleep,
> As soon as day's first beams do peep;
> That they may rise, and say their prayers,
> And not be caught in this world's cares."

Then he went on again, Too-whit! too-woo! shaking his solemn old head to and fro. He was a melancholy Owl; I think he must have been crossed in love.

Solomon thought this Owl very clever to roll out beautiful poetry like that, off-hand as it were. He asked the Owl again--

"Tell me, O wise Owl, why do you shake your very solemn old head?"

Said the Owl--

> "I shake my head, to let all know
> This world is but a fleeting show.
> Men's days are flying with quick wings;
> So take no joy in earthly things.
>
> "Yet men will fix their hearts below
> Upon the pleasures that must go.
> Their joy is gone when they are dead;
> And that is why I shake my head."

This touched King Solomon in a tender place, for he was himself rather fond of earthly delights. He sighed, and asked again--

"O most ancient and wise Owl! tell me why you never eat grain?"

Answered the Owl--

> "The bearded grain I do not eat,
> Because, when Adam ate some wheat,
> He was turned out of Paradise:
> So Adam's sin has made me wise.
>
> "If I should eat a single grain,
> The joys of heaven I should not gain.
> And so, to keep my erring feet,
> The bearded grain I never eat."

Thought Solomon to himself, "I don't remember reading that

story in Genesis, but perhaps he is right. I must look it up when I get home." Then he spoke to the Owl once more, and said--

"And now, good Owl, tell me why you drink no water at night?"

Said the Owl--

> "Since water all the world did drown
> In Noah's day, I will drink none.
> Were I to drink a single drop,
> My life would then most likely stop."

Solomon was delighted to find the Owl so wise. "O my Owl," said he, "all my life long I have been looking for a counsellor who had reasons to give for what he did; I have never found one until I found you. Now I beg you to come home with me to-morrow, and you shall be my chief counsellor, and whatever I purpose I will first ask your advice."

The Owl was equally delighted, and said, "Thank you." Thinking of the greatness that was to be his, the Owl stopped crying Too-whit! too-woo! and Solomon went to sleep.

The Camel's Neck

ONCE upon a time there was a very religious Camel; at least, he was religious after the fashion of his country, that is, he used to mortify his flesh by fasting, and scratch himself with thorns, and lie awake all night meditating upon the emptiness of the world. That is what men used to do in that country, in order to please their gods. One of these gods was very much pleased with the piety of the Camel; so one night, as the Camel was fasting, and saying over and over to himself, "Vanity of vanities, all is vanity," the god appeared before him. He was a curious-looking god, and he had four hands instead of two; but the Camel did not mind that, nor did he laugh; on the contrary, he went down on his knees and bowed before him.

"O Camel," said this god, "I have seen your fasting and heard your prayers; and I have come to reward you. Choose what boon you like, and it shall be yours."

"O mighty god, I should like to have a neck eight miles long."

The god answered, "Be it so!" and immediately the Camel felt his neck shooting out like a telescope, until it was eight miles long. It shot out so fast, that the Camel found it hard to escape running his head against the trees. However, he steered it successfully, barring a bump or two; and as by the time his neck stopped growing he was far out of sight of the god, he could not even say thank you.

Now perhaps you will wonder why this Camel wanted a neck so long as eight miles? I will tell you. The reason was, that for all his fastings and penances, he was a lazy Camel, and he wanted to graze without the trouble of walking about. And now he could easily graze for a distance of eight miles all round in a circle, without moving from the spot where he lay. But it was rather dangerous, though he thought nothing of that; for when his head was grazing a few miles away, the hunters might stick a spear into his body, or tie his legs together, without his seeing them.

All the summer the Camel had a fine time of it; he lay still and comfortable and sent his head foraging around, and strange to say, no harm happened to him. But before long the rainy season began. In the rainy season there are storms every day, and it rains cats and dogs. So when the rain began, the Camel wanted to keep dry, but he could not at first find a shed or a shelter eight miles long, or anything like it. At last he lit on a long winding cave that held most of his long neck. So he ran his neck into the cave, and lay still, with the rain pouring upon his body.

This was bad enough, but worse was to come. For it happened that in this cave lived a He-jackal and a She-jackal.

When the Jackals saw this extraordinary neck winding along their cave, they were frightened, and hid away.

"What is this snake?" said the He-jackal to his wife.

"Oh dear, I don't know!" whimpered his wife, "I never saw a snake like this."

They kept quiet, the head passed out of view into the inner part of the cave; then after a while, the creature lay still.

"Let us smell him!" said the He-jackal.

They smelt him. "He smells nice," said the She-jackal; "not a bit like a snake."

"Let us taste him!" said the He-jackal.

They took a bite; the Camel stirred restlessly. They took another bite, and liked that better still. They went on biting. The Camel curled round his head to see what was going on; but before the Camel's head could get back more than a mile or two, he grew so weak from loss of blood, that he could move no more, and he died.

So died the idle Camel, because the god granted him his foolish wish. Perhaps our wishes are often just as foolish, if we only knew it; and perhaps if they were fulfilled they would be the bane of us, as happened to the lazy and religious Camel.

The Quail and the Fowler

A FOWLER once caught a Quail. Said the Quail to the Fowler--

"O Fowler, I know four things that will be useful for you to know."

"What are they?" asked the Fowler.

"Well," said the Quail, "I don't mind telling you three of them now. The first is: Fast caught, fast keep; never let a thing go when once you have got it. The second is: He is a fool that believes everything he hears. And the third is this: It's of no use crying over spilt milk."

The Fowler thought these very sensible maxims. "And what is the fourth?" he asked.

"Ah," said the Quail, "you must set me free if you want to hear the fourth."

The Fowler, who was a simple fellow, set the Quail free. The Quail fluttered up into a tree, and said--

"I see you take no notice of what I tell you. Fast caught, fast keep, I said; and yet you have let me go."

"Why, so I have," said the Fowler, and scratched his head. He was a foolish Fowler, I think. "Well, never mind; what is the fourth thing? You promised to tell me, and I am sure an honourable Quail will never break his word."

"The fourth thing I have to tell you is this: In my inside is a beautiful diamond, weighing ten pounds. And if you had not let me go, you would have had that diamond, and you need never have done any more work in all your life."

"Oh dear, oh dear, what a fool I am!" cried the Fowler. He fell on his face, and clutched at the grass, and began to cry.

"Ha, ha, ha!" laughed the Quail. "He is a fool who believes everything he hears."

"Eh? what?" said the Fowler, and stopped crying.

"Do you think a little carcase like mine can hold a diamond as big as your head?" asked the Quail, roaring with laughter. "And even if it were true, where's the use of crying over spilt milk?"

The Quail spread his wings. "Good-bye," said he; "better luck next time, Fowler." And he flew away.

The Fowler sat up. "Well," said he, "that's true, sure enough." He got up and brushed the mud off his clothes. "If I have lost a Quail," said he, "I've learnt something." And he went home, a sadder but a wiser man.

The King of the Kites

A MOUSE one day met a Frog, whom he knew very well; but the Frog turned up his flat nose, and would not speak to him.

"Friend Frog," said the Mouse, "why are you so proud to-day?"

"Because I am King of the Kites," said Froggie.

You must not suppose that this means a paper kite with a tail. There is a kind of bird called a Kite; it is like a Hawk, only bigger. How absurd it was of this Frog, who could not even fly, to call himself the King of the Kites! And the Mouse was just as absurd, for he answered--

"Stuff and nonsense! I am King of the Kites!"

I don't know whether they really believed this themselves, or whether they were only trying to show off. Anyhow, both stuck to it stoutly, and a pretty quarrel was the result. The Mouse grew red in the face; and as for Froggie, he was nearly bursting with rage.

At last they agreed to refer the decision to a council. The council was made up of a Bat, a Squirrel, and a Parrot. The Parrot took the chair, because he was the biggest, and also because he could talk most, and was therefore thought to be wise.

"I vote for the Mouse," said the Bat; not that he knew anything about it, but you see a Bat is very like a Mouse, and he wanted to stand up for the family.

"And I," said the Squirrel, "vote for my friend Froggie." He knew nothing about it either, but he wanted to show that even a Squirrel has an opinion of his own.

So it fell to the Parrot to give the casting vote, and decide the matter. He took a long time to decide, about two hours; and while he was thinking, and the others were all intent to hear what he should say, down from the sky swooped a Kite; and the Kite stuck one claw into the Mouse's back, and one claw into the Frog, and carried them both away to his nest, and ate them for dinner.

So that was the end of the two Kings of the Kites. The other three creatures, in a great fright, made themselves scarce, lest the Kite should come back and eat them too.

The Jackal and the Camel

Once a Camel was grazing in a forest. He had a ring in his nose, as the custom is, and to the ring was tied a string, by which the Camel's master used to lead him about. As the Camel grazed, this leading-string became entangled in a bush, and the Camel could not get it loose. This misfortune so much confused the mind of the Camel that he did not know what to do.

Suddenly, as the Camel was struggling to get free from the bush, a Jackal appeared.

"Brother Jackal," said the Camel, "do please set me free from this bush."

"Brother Camel," said the Jackal, "I will set you free, only you must pay me for it. Do not the wise say, 'Even a brother will not serve thee for nothing'?"

"What shall I pay you, brother Jackal? I am a very poor Camel."

"You shall pay me," quoth the Jackal, "a pound of your flesh."

This was a hard condition, but there was nothing for it, "Better to lose a pound of my flesh," thought the Camel, "than lose my life." So he agreed to pay the Jackal a pound of flesh.

Then the Jackal set the Camel free, and the Camel sat down on the ground and said--

"I am ready; take your pound of flesh."
"Open your mouth, then," said the Jackal.
"Why?" asked the Camel.
"Because I choose to take my pound of flesh from your tongue."

This was a terrible blow. The Camel could not agree, because he knew that if his tongue were torn out, he was bound to die.

So he said, "I did not promise you my tongue."

"You did," said the Jackal.

"Don't tell lies," said the Camel; "where are your witnesses?"

Away trotted the Jackal to find a witness. First he asked the Lion if he would bear witness that he heard the Camel promise to give his tongue. He promised to give him the half of all he should get, as a reward.

"Go away," said the King of Beasts; "I am a Lion, not a liar." Then he asked the Tiger, but the Tiger said--

"I don't care for Camel's meat, so it isn't worth my while."

And so the Jackal tried one beast after another, but none of them would help him, until he came to the Wolf.

"Friend Wolf," said the Jackal, "if you will only swear that you heard the Camel promise me his tongue, you shall have half."

"Half a tongue?" quoth the Wolf; "that's poor provender."

"No, no," said the Jackal, "half the Camel. Don't you see that if we tear out his tongue, the Camel will soon bleed to death."

"True, so he will," said the Wolf. "Well, I agree."

So the Wolf and the Jackal went back to the Camel, and the Wolf said, raising his right forepaw to heaven--

"I swear by heaven that I heard this Camel promise to give his tongue to this Jackal."

Of course this was a lie, and they all knew it; but the Camel did not like to appear mean, and besides, they were two to one.

"Very well," said the Camel; "come and take it." The Camel opened his mouth wide. The Jackal put his head in the Camel's mouth, and as he did so, the Camel curled his tongue backward, so that the Jackal could not
reach it.

The Jackal pulled his head out again, and said to the Wolf--

"My mouth is too small, you try now--you have a big gape."

Then the Wolf put his head in the Camel's mouth. The Camel curled his tongue back and back, and the Wolf pushed in his head further and further; at last all the Wolf's head was inside.

Then the Camel snapped his jaws together upon the Wolf's neck.

"O Daddy Camel," said the Wolf, half throttled; "what is this?"

"This," said the Jackal, rolling up the whites of his eyes to the sky in a most pious fashion; "this is the result of telling a lie." The Camel said nothing at all, but simply throttled the Wolf to death, and the Jackal ran away.

I think you will agree with me, that the Jackal, who made the Wolf tell a lie, was wickeder than the Wolf who told it; but yet he laughed at the Wolf, and got off himself scot-free. That often happens in this world; but we will hope that some other time his sin was bound to
find him out.

The Wise Old Shepherd

Once upon a time, a snake went out of his hole to take an airing. He crawled about, greatly enjoying the scenery and the fresh whiff of the breeze, until, seeing an open door, he went in. Now this door was the door of the palace of the King, and inside was the King himself, with all his courtiers.

Imagine their horror at seeing a huge Snake crawling in at the door. They all ran away except the King, who felt that his rank forbade him to be a coward, and the King's son. The King called out for somebody to come and kill the Snake; but this horrified them still more, because in that country the people believed it to be wicked to kill any living thing, even snakes, and scorpions, and wasps. So the courtiers didnothing, but the young Prince obeyed his father, and killed the Snake with his stick.

After a while the Snake's wife became anxious, and set out in search of her husband. She too saw the open door of the palace, and in she went. O horror! there on the floor lay the body of her husband, all covered with blood, and quite dead. No one saw the Snake's wife crawl in; she inquired from a white ant what had happened, and when she found that the young Prince had killed her husband, she made a vow, that as he had made her a widow, so she would make his wife a widow.

That night, while all the world was asleep, the Snake crept into the Prince's bedroom, and coiled around his neck. The Prince slept on, and when he awoke in the morning, he was surprised to find his neck encircled with the coils of a Snake. He was afraid to stir, so there he remained, until the Prince's mother became anxious, and went to see what was the matter. When she entered his room, and saw him in this plight, she gave a loud shriek, and ran off to tell the King.

"Call the archers," said the King. The archers came, and the King told them to go into the Prince's room, and shoot the Snake that was coiled about his neck. They were so clever, that they could easily do this without hurting the Prince at all.

In came the archers in a row, fitted the arrows to the bows, the bows were raised ready to shoot, when, on a sudden, from the Snake there issued a voice, which spoke as follows:--

"O archers! wait, and hear me before you shoot. It is not fair to carry out the sentence before you have heard the case. Is not this good law, an eye for an eye, and a tooth for a tooth? Is it not so, O King?"

"Yes," replied the King, "that is our law."

"Then," said the Snake, "I plead the law. Your son has made me a widow, so it is fair and right that I should make his wife a widow."

"That sounds right enough," said the King, "but right and law are not always the same thing. We had better ask somebody who knows."

They asked all the judges, but none of them could tell the law of the matter. They shook their heads, and said they would look up all their law-books, and see whether anything of the sort had ever happened before, and if so, how it had been decided. That is the way judges used to decide cases in that country, though I daresay it sounds to you a very funny way. It looked as if they had not much sense in their own heads, and perhaps that was true. The upshot of all was, that not a judge would give any opinion; so the King sent messengers all over the country-side, to see if they could find somebody somewhere who knew something.

One of these messengers found a party of five Shepherds, who were sitting upon a hill and trying to decide a quarrel of their own. They gave their opinions so freely, and in language so very strong, that the King's messenger said to himself, "Here are the men for us. Here are five men, each with an opinion of his own, and all different." Post-haste he scurried back to the King, and told him he had found at last some one ready to judge the knotty point.

So the King and the Queen, and the Prince and the Princess, and all the courtiers, got on horseback, and away they galloped to the hill whereupon the five Shepherds were sitting, and the Snake too went with them, coiled round the neck of the Prince.

When they got to the Shepherds' hill, the Shepherds were dreadfully frightened. At first they thought that the strangers were a gang of robbers; and when they saw that it was the King, their next thought was that one of their misdeeds had been found out, and each of them began thinking what was the last thing he had done, and wondering, was it that? But the King and his Court got off their horses, and said good-day in the most civil way. So the Shepherds felt their minds set at ease again. Then the King said--

"Worthy Shepherds, we have a question to put to you, which not all the judges in all the courts of my city have been able to solve. Here is my son, and here, as you see, is a Snake coiled round his neck. Now, the husband of this Snake came creeping into my palace hall, and my son the Prince killed him; so this Snake, who is the wife of the other, says that as my son has made her a widow, so she has a right to widow my son's wife. What do you think about it?"

The first Shepherd said, "I think she is quite right, my lord King. If any one made my wife a widow, I would pretty soon do the same to him."

This was brave language, and the other Shepherds shook their heads and looked fierce. But the King was puzzled, and could not quite understand it. You see, in the first place, if the man's wife were a widow, the man
would be dead; and then it is hard to see how he could do anything. So to make sure, the King asked the second Shepherd whether that was his opinion too?

"Yes," said the second Shepherd; "now the Prince has killed the Snake, the Snake has a right to kill the Prince, if he can."

But that was not of much use either, as the Snake was as dead as a door-nail. So the King passed on to the third.

"I agree with my mates," said the third Shepherd, "because, you see, a Prince is a Prince, but then a Snake is a Snake."

That was quite true, they all admitted; but it did not seem to help the matter much. Then the King asked the fourth Shepherd to say what he thought.

The fourth Shepherd said, "An eye for an eye, and a tooth for a tooth; so I think a widow should be a widow, if so be she don't marry again."

By this time the poor King was so puzzled that he hardly knew whether he stood on his head or his heels. But there was still the fifth Shepherd left, the oldest and wisest of them all; and the fifth Shepherd said--

"O King, I should like to ask two questions."

"Ask twenty, if you like," said the King. He did not promise to answer them, so he could afford to be generous.

"First, I ask the Princess how many sons she has?"
"Four," said the Princess.
"And how many sons has Mistress Snake here?"
"Seven," said the Snake.
"Then," said the old Shepherd, "it will be quite fair for Mistress Snake to kill his Highness the Prince, when her Highness the Princess has had three sons more."

"I never thought of that," said the Snake. "Good-bye, King, and all you good people. Send a message when the Princess has had three more sons, and you may count upon me--I will not fail you." So saying, she uncoiled from the Prince's neck and slid away among the grass.

The King and the Prince and everybody shook hands with the wise old Shepherd, and went home again. And as the Princess never had any more sons at all, she and the Prince lived happily for many years; and if they are not dead they are living still.

Beware of Bad Company

A Beautiful young Swan lived by a beautiful lake. All day long he used to sail gracefully over the water, curving his neck to look at his own image, or pluming his white wings; and when he was tired, he would go to his nest in the rushes, and sleep, or play with his brothers and sisters.

In a tree above that lake was a Crow. You know that Crows are dirty birds, and they feed on offal and refuse, and people dislike them; but the Swan was white and clean. Still, strange as it may seem, this Swan struck up a fast friendship with the Crow. His mother and father begged him to keep out of bad company, but he would not listen to them. He had done better to keep to his own kind, but wilful will have his way, and the Swan was sorry for it too late.

One day the Crow said to his friend the Swan, "Come, old boy, let us go and have some fun."

"I'm your Swan," says the other, and away they flew.
They came to a tree, and under the tree was a very pious man, saying his prayers.

"Here's a joke," said the Crow. "Now we shall see sport."

He picked up a lump of mud from the ground, and flew up into the tree, and then he dropped the mud, splash, on the pious man's head.

This interrupted his prayers, and he could not help feeling angry, although he was so pious. So up got he, and looked about to see who had done the mischief.

By this time the mischievous Crow had flown off, and he was caw-caw-cawing on another tree, out of reach. But the Swan sat still: he was not learned in mischief, and he did not know what to do. Then the pious man looked up into the tree, and saw the Swan sitting there, so of course he thought it was the Swan who had dropped a piece of mud on his head. He had a big catapult with him, so he put a stone in his catapult, and slick! he shot the Swan.

Down fell the Swan with a great thud. He felt that his end was near, and how sorry he was now that he had had anything to do with the bad Crow. However, it was too late now to be sorry, so he began to sing. They say
that Swans never sing in all their life, but when they are about to die they sing beautifully; and this is what the Swan sang to the pious man:--

"I am no Crow, as you must know,
But a Swan that lived by a lovely lake;
With bad companions I would go,
And now I die for a bad friend's sake."

Then the Swan died, and the pious man finished his prayers.

The Foolish Wolf

Wolf and an Ass were great friends, and they spent most of their time playing at an original game of their own. The game was easy enough to learn; you could play it yourselves; and it was this. First the Ass used to run away from the Wolf as hard as he could, and the Wolf used to follow; and then the Wolf would run as hard as he could from the Ass, and the Ass would follow.

One day, as the Wolf was running away full tilt from the Ass, a Boy saw them.

"Ha, ha, ha," said the Boy, "what a coward that Wolf is, to run away from an Ass." He thought, you see, that the Wolf was afraid of being eaten by the Ass.

The Wolf heard him, and was very angry. He stopped short, and said to the Boy--

"So you think I am a coward, little Boy? You shall rue the word.

I'm brave enough to eat you, as you shall find out this very night; for I will come and carry you off from your home."

If the Wolf was no coward, at least he was a foolish Wolf to tell the Boy if he meant to carry him off, as I think you will agree with me.

The Boy went home to tell his mother. "Mother," said he, "a Wolf is coming to-night to carry me off."

"Oh, never mind if he does," said the Boy's mother, "he won't hurt you."

The Boy did not feel quite so sure about that, for he had seen sharp teeth in the mouth of the Wolf. So he chose out a big and sharp stone, and put it in his pocket. Why he did not hide, I can't tell you, for he never told me; but my private opinion is, he was almost as foolish as the Wolf.

Well, when night came, the Boy's mother went to bed, and she was soon snoring, but the Boy stayed up to wait for the Wolf. About ten o'clock came a knock at the door.

"Come in," said the Boy.
The Wolf opened the door, and came in, and says he, "Now, Boy, you must come along with me."

"All right," says the Boy, "mother doesn't mind."

I have never been able to understand why his mother did not mind, but perhaps he was a very naughty Boy, and she was glad to get rid of him. If he did nothing but pull his sisters' hair, and put spiders down their necks, he was just as well out of the house, I think.

So the Boy got on the Wolf's back, and the Wolf trotted off briskly to his den. Then the Wolf thought to himself, "I have had my dinner, and I don't want any Boy to-night. Suppose I leave him for to-morrow, and go for a spin with my friend the Jackass."

So he left the Boy in his den, and off he went after the Jackass.

What makes me think more than ever that he was a foolish Wolf, is that he never even tied the Boy's legs together. So when the Wolf was gone, the Boy went out of the den, and climbed up a tree.

In an hour or two back came the Wolf, ready for bed. He looked in at the mouth of the den, but no Boy.

"Where on earth has that Boy got to?" said he; "I left him here safe and sound." It never occurred to this Wolf that legs can walk, and Boys can climb trees. He felt very anxious, and as many people do when their wits are puzzled, he opened his mouth wide.

The Boy saw him standing at the opening of the den, with his mouth wide open, so he pulled the sharp stone out of his pocket, and threw it in. This Boy was a very good shot with a stone, and the stone went straight into the Wolf's inside, and cut his inside so much that he died.

Then the Boy climbed down from the tree, and he was at home in time for breakfast. I don't know whether his mother was pleased to see him or not; but there he was, and there he stayed, and if he has not gone away, he is there still.

Reflected Glory

There was a Shepherd who owned a multitude of goats. Among these was one Goat, weak and lame. You might suppose that the shepherd took especial care of this lame Goat, but not he; on the contrary, he beat him and bullied him, and made his whole life a misery.

A time came when the lame Goat could stand it no longer. So watching his chance, he gave his master the slip, and into the forest and far away. As he hobbled along, he trembled to think of the ferocious beasts that
the forest was full of; but even to be devoured by an evil beast was better far than to be for ever beaten.

The lame Goat made up his mind that the only way by which he could save his life was to gain the protection of some powerful beast. So he kept his eyes open as he hobbled along; and, by-and-by, what should he see but a dark cave, and at the mouth of the cave, a Lion's footprints. Now a Lion was just the beast the Goat wanted, for to begin with, he is the King of Beasts, and all the other beasts fear him; and then, too, he is a noble beast, and if he passes his word he will never break it. Of course, it might be that the Lion would eat our Goat first, and ask questions afterwards; but the Goat had to take his chance of that.

The upshot of it was, that the lame Goat sat down by the Lion's den, and waited.

By-and-by, trippity trip, trippity trip, and up came a Jackal. Said the Jackal to the Goat, "God bless you, Gaffer Goat, you'll be the first food that has passed my lips this many a day."

"Dear grandson," said the Goat, "God bless you too. I'm here to be eaten, that is true enough; but I'm meat for your betters. He whose footprints you see here has bidden me wait until he wants me."

The Jackal looked at the footprints, and saw they were a Lion's. "Aha," thought he, "let sleeping dogs lie. If I eat the Lion's meat, the Lion will devour my cubs." Then he went away sorrowful.

A little while, and trappity trap, trappity trap, up came a Wolf. Quoth the Wolf--

"Well met, Nuncle Goat; you make my mouth water. A five days' fast is sauce for the dinner."

"Well met, my dear nephew," says the lame Goat. "But you had better leave me alone. I'm food for your betters. Look upon these footprints, and let me tell you that he who made them has bidden me wait here until he is hungry."

"Oho," said the Wolf, "a Lion. Who tackles the strong will not live long. If I eat King Lion's meat, King Lion will make a meal of my cubs." Away went the Wolf, trappity trap, trappity trap.

A little while more, and swish, swish, swish, the Lion himself came stalking slowly along, whisking away the flies with his tail. When he saw the Goat sitting beside his den, says he--

"Friend Goat, what want you here? Are you anxious to make a meal for me?"

"O King Lion," said the Goat, bowing before him very humbly, "here I have been sitting these two hours, and wolves and jackals came to eat me; but the sight of your footprints was safety for me: I told them I was yours, and they took to their heels for fear. Now eat me if you
will; for yours I am."

Then the Lion said, "O Goat, if you have called yourself mine, never will I devour you. I will see to it that you are well treated."

Then the Lion went out and found an Elephant, who greeted him with the greatest respect. "Elephant," said the Lion, "I want you to do something for me."

"Speak on," said the Elephant, "do it I will."

The Lion said, "There is a poor lame Goat has thrown himself on my mercy, and I have thought of a plan by which he can be fed. If you will suffer him to mount on your back, then while you go grazing about, he can browse upon the young shoots of the trees as you pass under."

"That is a good idea," said the Elephant, "and I'll do it for you willingly, and indeed anything else in my power."

If the Lion was pleased at the kindness of the Elephant, more pleased was the lame Goat; and a happy life was his from that day. Never again was he beaten by a cruel goatherd: but he fed on the fat of the land, and lived to a green old age; and I hope we may be half as happy as he was.

The Cat and the Sparrows

here was once a pair of Sparrows that lived in a tree. They used to hop about all over the place, picking up seeds or anything they could find to eat. One day, when they came back with their pickings, the Cock had found some rice, and the Hen a few lentils. They put it all in an earthen pot, and then proceeded to cook their dinner. Then they divided the mess into two equal parts.

The Cock was rather greedy, so he would not wait while his wife put out the fire and got ready to join in the meal. No! he gobbled up his share at once, before she could begin.

When at last the poor Hen came up, her greedy mate would not let her rest even then. "Go and get me a drink of water," said he quite rudely.

She was a very kind wife, so without taking any notice of his rudeness, off she went for the water.

While she was gone the Cock-sparrow's eyes fell on his wife's share of the dinner. "Ah," thought he, "how I should like another bit! Well, why shouldn't I have it? A man does all the work, and women don't want much to eat at any time." So without any more ado, he just set to, and gobbled up his wife's share.

Back came the Hen-sparrow with a drink of water for her husband. When he had drunk it up (and I am afraid he forgot to say thank you), she turned round to look for her dinner. Lo and behold! there was none. What could have become of it? As she was wondering, she happened to look at her husband; he looked so guilty that there could be no manner of doubt where her dinner was.

"You greedy bird," said she, "why have you eaten my dinner?"

"I haven't touched your dinner," said the Cock angrily.
"I'm sure you have," said she, "or you would not look so guilty. Why, you are actually blushing." And so indeed he was; the tip of his beak was quite red.

However, he still denied it, and grew angrier and angrier, as people do when they know they are in the wrong. They had a terrible quarrel. At last the Hen-sparrow said, "Well, I know a way to find out whether you are telling lies or not. You come along with me." And she made him go with her to the well.

Across the top of the well she stretched a piece of string, and she sat on the middle of the string, and began to chirp, "If I am telling lies, I pray I may fall in." But though she sat there a long time, chirping away, she did not fall in.

Then came the Cock-sparrow's turn. He perched on the string and began to chirrup, "If I am telling lies, may I fall into the well;" but hardly had he got the words out of his mouth, when--splash! down he went.

Then the Hen was very sorry that she had proposed this plan; she began to weep and cheep, and said--"Alas, alas, why didn't I leave it alone? What does it matter if he eats my dinner, so long as I have my dear husband? Now I have killed him by my folly."

Just at that moment up came a Cat.
"What's the matter?" said the Cat.

"Cheep, cheep, cheep," went the Hen-sparrow. "My husband has fallen into the well, and I don't know how to get him out."

"If I get him out," said the Cat, "will you let me eat him?"
"Of course you may," said the Hen-sparrow.
So the Cat climbed down, and pulled out the Cock-sparrow. When she had brought him to the edge of the well, said she,

"Now I'm going to eat him as you promised."

"Oh, all right," said the Hen. "But stop a minute, your mouth is dirty. I am sure you have been eating mice. Now haven't you?"

"Why, yes," said the Cat, "so I have."
"Well," said the Hen-sparrow, "you must get yourself clean. We birds are clean creatures, and you must positively wash your mouth before you begin."

Away went the Cat, and washed her mouth clean, and came back again.

The Hen-sparrow looked at her carefully. "You have not washed your whiskers," said she; "they are still dirty."

The Cat went obediently and washed her whiskers.

Meanwhile the Cock-sparrow had been sitting on the edge of the well in the sun, and by this time his feathers were quite dry. So his Hen chirped to him, "Now, dear, you can fly, let's be off." And off they flew together, and the Cat was left licking her chops and wishing she had not been such a fool.

The Foolish Fish

A Fish was once flapping and flopping on the sand by the banks of a river. She was a lady Fish--how she got there I don't know; but she had been better to stay at home, as you shall hear. Well, she flapped away on the sand, and couldn't get off; she began to feel very dry. A man came by, riding upon a horse. "O Man," shouted the Fish, "do carry me back to the water again, or I shall be dried up and die."

"No, no," said the Man, "not I, indeed! You are a she, and I have had so much bother with shes in my life that I shall keep clear of you."

"O dear good Man!" cried the Fish, "do please help me, and I will promise not to behave badly; I'll be as nice as any man could be. Just think! if you leave me here, I shall dry into a stick, or somebody will come along and eat me."

The Man scratched his head, and wondered what he ought to do; but at last he took pity on the Fish, and got down off his horse. Then he picked up the Fish and put her on his shoulder, and walked down to the water. "Now then," said he, "in with you."

"Take me into deep water," said the Fish; "this won't do for me." So the good-natured fellow took her and waded into the water till he was neck-deep. Then the Fish opened her mouth wide, and said--

"Now I'm going to eat you! I'll teach you to say nasty things about women."

That was a nice way of showing gratitude to the Man, wasn't it? I wonder the Man did not eat the Fish, instead of the Fish eating him. But I am afraid the Man was rather stupid. It never occurred to him that he might eat the Fish, and all he did was to scratch his head again. "That's not fair," said he; "I saved your life, and now you want to eat me. We must find some one to decide between us, and say which is right."

"All right," said the Fish; "take me up on your shoulder again, and let us find somebody."

So the Man took her up on his shoulder again, and out of the water came he. On the bank of the river grew a Crab-apple Tree, and the Man appealed to this Tree to decide their dispute. "O Tree," said he, "this Fish was lying on the sand, and I saved her life, and now she wants to eat me. Do you think that is right?"

"Of course!" said the Tree--whose temper was as crabbed as his apples--"of course! Why not? You men are always doing mischief. Here am I, an innocent Crab-apple Tree, and people come along and cut off my branches to shade themselves from the sun. I call that cool!"

"Well," said the Man, "they want to be cool, and that's why they cut your branches off."

"Don't be a fool," squeaked the Crab-apple Tree; "you know what I mean. So as you do all this damage to us, we are right to do all we can to hurt you, and therefore this Fish has a right to eat you if she chooses."

"Come along," said the Fish, as she opened her mouth; "jump in!"

"Wait a bit," said the Man, "we must try somebody else. I feel sure there is something wrong with this judgment." The Fish did not wish to ask anybody else, but she had to agree, because they were on dry land. So they went along until they saw an Elephant.

"O Elephant!" cried the Man, "do you see this Fish? I saved her life, and now she wants to eat me. Do you think this is right?"

"Right?" said the Elephant, "I should rather think so! Why, you men are horrid brutes, always making us carry half-a-dozen of you about on our backs, or prodding us with a spike, or something nasty. Eat you up? I only wish _I_ could eat you up, and I would do it too, but nature makes me eat leaves, and you are too tough for me to digest."

So there was no comfort to be had from the Elephant.

The Fish opened her mouth wider than ever, for she was getting hungry, and said, "Now then, look sharp--in with you!"

The Man was in despair. What was he to do? "Give me one more chance," said he, "and if they all say the same, then you shall eat me."

He looked round, and not far off he saw a Jackal. "Friend Jackal," he called out; "I say, Jackal! Stop a minute, I want to ask you something."

"All right," said the Jackal, "ask away."

"This Fish," said the Man, "was flip-flap-flopping on the sand and gasping for breath, and I saved her life; and then as soon as she got safe back into the water again, she wanted to eat me. Do you think that's right?"

"Hm," said the Jackal, "I don't quite understand. Where was the Fish?"

"Lying on the sand, you booby," said the Fish, getting angry.

"How?" asked the Jackal.

"Why," said the Fish, "what does that matter, I should like to know?"

"Can't understand," said the Jackal, looking stupidly all round and then up at the sky.

"Well," said the Fish, angrier than ever, "all you are asked to do, is to say whether or no I am to eat this Man. Can't you do that without all this bother?"

"No," said the Jackal.

"Oh dear," said the Fish, "what a stupid you must be! All right then,
come along, and we'll show you." So she made the Man take her

on his shoulder again, and carry her to the place where she had been lying on the sand.

"That's the place," said she.

The Jackal was not satisfied yet, but he must needs see how she lay. So the Man put her down on the sand, and the Fish began flip-flap-flopping again.

"Now then," said the Jackal to the Man, "up on the horse with you, and be off! What does the Fish matter to you? Let her die, she deserves no better."

The Man thought this a good idea, so he got up on his horse, and off, and was more resolved than ever to keep clear of women.

But the Fish was very angry at being tricked so neatly. "You shall pay for this!" she gasped to the Jackal; "I'll come and eat you in your den."

"All right, you may try," said the Jackal, "but I fancy you will get eaten yourself." And so saying, away he scampered.

The Fish flapped and flopped, until somehow or other she managed to flap herself into the river.

After this the Fish used to sit by the roots of a fig-tree which went down into the river, with her mouth gaping, in the hope that something might fall in. The Jackal used to come down to this place to drink, and one day, as he was drinking, the Fish caught him tight by the leg.

"Oh you silly Fish," said the Jackal, "why didn't you catch my leg?

You have got hold of the wrong thing," said he; "there's my leg, if you want it," pointing to the root of the fig-tree. The foolish Fish believed she had made a mistake, and let go the Jackal's leg, and took a good bite of the root. The Jackal laughed, and scampered away, crying, "Oh what a fool you are! You don't know wood from meat!"

"Never mind," said the Fish, "next time it will be my turn, and then we shall see. I'll come and eat you in your den."

Next day, when the Jackal had gone into the forest to find food, our friend the Fish jumped out of the water, and went roll, roll, rolling into the forest, until she came to the den of the Jackal; and inside the door of the Jackal's den she stood on her tail, waiting for him to come back. By-and-by back came the Jackal, sure enough; but Jackals are very cunning creatures, and he came up slinking quietly, and saw the Fish before the Fish saw him. So he called out in a loud voice, "Den, Den!"

No answer. Again he called out, "Den, Den!" This time the Fish thought that the Den was no doubt accustomed to reply when the Jackal called to it. Perhaps it was shy because she was present. Anyhow she thought she had better answer, so she called out in return, "Well, well!"

"You there?" asked the Jackal.
"Yes, I'm here all right," answered the Fish.
"Just stop a minute," said the Jackal, "and I'll be back directly."

Away he ran, and the Fish crept inside the hole, and hid. The Jackal ran about gathering dry leaves, and with the leaves he made a little pile at the mouth of his hole. Then he went to a fire which some traveller had left smouldering, and seizing a brand, he brought it and set light to the leaves at the mouth of the cave. The fire soon burned up.

"Is that nice, dear Den?" asked the Jackal.

"Very nice, thank you," said the Fish, who thought she must go on pretending.

"I'll soon make you warm," said the Jackal, and he piled on more fuel. It began to get very hot.

"That's enough now," said the Fish.

"No, no, Den dear," said the cunning Jackal, laughing to himself. More and more leaves he piled on the top of the fire. One side of the Fish got so hot that she turned the other. Then it got hotter and hotter, and soon the Fish expired. When the fire went out, the Jackal looked into the cave, and there was the Fish, done on both sides crisp and brown. He sat down on his haunches, and gobbled her up in a trice, and he never had a nicer dinner. That was the end of the foolish and ungrateful Fish.

The Clever Goat

A Shepherd was feeding his flock on the hills; and as they were going home again in the evening, one of the goats lagged behind. Now, this Goat was very old, and goats are not like men, for the older they grow the wiser they become. So this Goat, being very old indeed, was also very wise. There was a very nice clump of grass by the wayside, and the wise old Goat said to herself, "Here is the nicest grass I have seen for a long time. I'm not hungry, because I have been eating all day; but I daresay I shall soon be hungry again, so I had better eat it while I can get it." And accordingly she set to work, and very soon she had eaten it all up. Then she trotted off homeward.

As the old Goat went merrily trotting along, with her eyes on the ground, suddenly she looked up--and lo and behold! a huge Wolf sitting on a stump, and staring at her hungrily! What was she to do? To escape was impossible. She pulled her wits together, and began--

"Oh, my dear Mr. Wolf!" cried she, "how delighted I am to see you. I have been looking for you all day, and now I've found you at last."

The Wolf was so utterly astonished that he had not a word to say at first. But after a while, he found his tongue, and thus said he--

"My good Goat, you must be out of your senses. Why, I'm accustomed to feed on goats, and here you say you are glad to see me. Who ever heard of a creature so foolish as to throw itself into the jaws of death of its own free will?"

"Ah," replied the Goat, "you don't know my Shepherd, that's quite clear. He is the kindest man in the world, and he has a special weakness for you. He was talking of you only this morning, and saying that he owes you a good turn for not gobbling up any of his sheep, though it is ever so long since he began to feed them in your forest. So he has sent me to you as a token of his esteem. I'm an old Goat, you see, and not much use
to him now. 'No *ifs* and *buts*,' says he to me--'off with you, and let kind Mr. Wolf eat you for his dinner.' And so here I am. And indeed, you must not suppose I am here against my will; not at all. I could not think of disobeying our good Shepherd. And, if I did, he could sell me to the butcher, to have my throat cut, and be eaten by horrid beasts of men, who have only two legs to bless themselves with. I assure you, I much prefer being eaten by a noble four-legged gentleman like yourself."

Our Wolf was still so surprised that he could find nothing to say; and the Goat went on--

"Do not think, dear sir, that I am flattering you. Look at me and judge if a respectable old Goat of my age, and at the point of death--for I see you licking your chops--whether, I say, such a one would dare to tell lies. But, Mr. Wolf, there is one reason why I shall be sorry to die. You may not have heard of it, but it is true nevertheless that I am a famous songster, and it will be indeed a pity that a gift so rare should be lost. Will you do me one last favour, and let me sing you a song before I die? I am sure it will delight you, and you will enjoy eating me all the more afterwards."

The Wolf was very much pleased at the Goat's politeness. "Well," said he, "since you are so kind as to offer, I should like to hear what you can do in the way of music."

"All right," said our Goat, "just sit down on that hillock yonder, and I'll stay here; it won't sound so nice if I am too near you."

The Wolf trotted off to the hillock, and sat down, and waited for the Goat to begin her song. The Goat opened her mouth, and uttered a loud "Baa-baa-baa!"

"Is that all?" asked the Wolf. He was rather disappointed, but he did not say so, for fear of being thought an ignorant lout. "Oh no," said the Goat, "that was only tuning up, to get the pitch." Then she cried again, "Baa-baa-baa," louder than before.

Meanwhile the Shepherd was not far off, and he heard this loud Baa-baa of one of his goats. "Hullo," thought he, "what's up, I wonder?" and set off running in the direction of the sound. Just as the Wolf was getting impatient, and the Goat was opening her mouth for another Baa-baa, up came the Shepherd, behind the Wolf. Thwack, thwack, thwack! came his stick on the stupid Wolf, and with a groan the Wolf turned over and died on the spot. The Shepherd and his wise old Goat trudged happily home to the sheepfold, and after that the Goat took good care to keep with the flock.

www.ingramcontent.com/pod-product-compliance
Lightning Source LLC
Chambersburg PA
CBHW051808130726
47987CB00003B/1156